RIDG

Making Waves

Bernadette Kelly

Raintree is an imprint of Capstone Global Library Limited,
a company incorporated in England and Wales having its
registered office at 7 Pilgrim Street, London, EC4V 6LB –
Registered company number: 6695582

To contact Raintree, please email myorders@raintreepublishers.co.uk.

First published in Australia by Black Dog Books in 2006
Copyright © Bernadette Kelly 2006
First published in the United Kingdom in 2013
The moral rights of the proprietor have been asserted.

Printed and bound in China

Main cover photograph reproduced with permission
of Shutterstock/© Oleg Zabielin. Background image reproduced with
permission of Shutterstock/© gkuna.

ISBN 978 1 406 26674 0 (paperback)
17 16 15 14 13
10 9 8 7 6 5 4 3 2 1

British Library Cataloguing in Publication Data
A full catalogue record for this book is available from the British Library.

Making Waves

Bernadette Kelly

"There it is!" I called out from the back seat of the Moriarty family's 4×4.

"What?" said Reese Moriarty, my best friend, turning around.

I pointed to a sign directly ahead. "Seahorse Stables," I read aloud. Underneath, in smaller letters, the sign read, "Beachside Holiday Camp. Bring Your Horse."

I let out a long, slow breath as Mrs Moriarty slowed the car and turned at the sign. I had been looking forward to this trip for weeks now. The sight of the sign suddenly made it all real.

I wriggled in my seat, impatient to be out of the car. It had been a long trip. Reese and her mum had picked me up early, and we'd left Ridgeview that morning while it was still dark.

The car began a slow climb into wooded hills, along twisting, narrow roads. The roads were edged by a cliff face on one side. On the other, there was a sheer drop over scattered boulders to the sea.

The constant winding began to make my stomach churn. I tried not to look out of the window as the car approached each dangerous curve.

In the horse trailer behind the car were Reese's handsome grey gelding, Jefferson, and my own striking chestnut horse, Bobby. I hoped the two horses were feeling better than I was. Riding in the car for a long time always made me feel sick to my stomach.

"How's it going back there, Annie?" asked Mrs Moriarty.

"I'm okay, thanks," I said, with a weak smile.

"Don't worry," Reese said. "We'll be there soon."

Finally, the car rolled along the white gravel driveway of Seahorse Stables. The driveway opened up to reveal dozens of small yards, several sheds, and a small brick house with a tiled roof. Some of the yards had horses in them, and some were empty.

There were people everywhere. Most of the kids my age were dressed in jodhpurs, riding boots, and T-shirts. Some were standing around in groups, talking, while others were taking care of the horses in the paddocks, lugging water buckets and filling hay nets.

"Matt and Austin are here," said Reese,

leaning forward in her seat.

I picked out Matt Snyder and Austin Ryan –
two friends from my own riding club – standing
with some other people I didn't know.

As soon as the car stopped, Reese and I
jumped out and opened the trailer door. While
we backed out first Bobby, then Jefferson, Mrs
Moriarty pulled our bags and riding gear from
the back of the 4×4.

Reese and I headed over to the boys, leading
the horses behind us.

"Hi," Austin greeted us. "We've been here for
hours. Mr Snyder dropped us off. We've saved
you a couple of yards next to our horses."

A smiling young man stepped forward. "I'm
Pete Harper, and this is my sister, Hannah.
Welcome to Seahorse Stables."

Pete was tall. His wavy brown hair was long,
almost to his shoulders. His round, rimless glasses

and grey-green eyes made him look a little bit like an owl. I liked him right away. Hannah was shorter, with cropped dark hair. Her eyes were a startling bright blue.

The pair didn't look remotely related. Mrs Moriarty joined the group and introduced herself to Pete and Hannah, then handed Hannah a large envelope.

"I signed the disclaimer forms," said Mrs Moriarty. "There's one from Annie's parents, too."

"Come on," said Austin. "I'll show you where to put the horses."

We followed Austin.

I breathed in the salty sea air. "What's a disclaimer form?" I asked Reese.

"It's for insurance," explained Reese. "Basically it just says that we know that horse riding is a dangerous sport and we won't hold Pete or Hannah responsible if we fall off and hurt ourselves."

"Good thing they added that," I said with a laugh. "They must have been watching me practice lately." I knew how easy it was to fall off, although luckily, I had never been seriously hurt.

The square-shaped yards were built in two long lines that butted up against each other.

"I saved four yards for Ridgeview so our horses could stay together and not get lonely," Austin said.

"Cool," I said. "Bobby will love that."

Austin led me to an empty yard next to his own horse, a bay mare called Cruise.

Reese walked Jefferson around to the yard that backed up to Bobby's, beside Matt's Appaloosa, Bullet. If they wanted to, all four horses could socialize across the fence just by standing in the shared corner.

Mrs Moriarty parked the trailer alongside a line of others and unhitched it from the car. Then she walked over to the yards. She frowned as she looked at the rickety wooden rails of the paddocks.

"These yards have seen better days," she said, turning back to us. "Remember to check on your horses once in a while, okay, girls?"

"Sure, Mum," said Reese. "But don't worry. Even if they did get out, I don't think Jefferson and Bobby would go far from the other horses." Reese pointed to the enormous trees hanging over the paddocks. "At least the trees will give them some shade."

"Hmmm. Well, your gear is in the trailer," said Mrs Moriarty. "Make sure you keep it all together, and put it away when you're done every day. I don't want things getting lost or left behind."

With that final parting piece of advice, Mrs

Moriarty hugged us both. "See you both on Wednesday afternoon. Have fun!"

"We will," Reese said. "Love you, Mum."

I leaned back on a paddock rail, making it wobble dangerously. I stroked my horse's neck. "We're going to have so much fun," I agreed.

Once the horses were fed and watered, Hannah showed Reese and me to a cabin. It was one of a dozen small cabins dotted around the property.

Inside the cabin were two sets of bunk beds. A neatly folded pair of purple and white striped pyjamas lay on top of an unrolled sleeping bag on one of the top bunks.

"One of your cabinmates has already arrived," said Hannah. "We got a phone call from the other one. She's arriving after lunch."

Hannah pointed to the wall across from the beds, which was completely taken up by lockers. "You can put your things in the lockers. Toilets and showers are over there."

She pointed through the open door to a brick building. It had two doors. One door had a sign that read "Colts." The other had a sign that read "Fillies."

I laughed. "Cute," I said.

Hannah smiled. "When you're done unpacking, come over to the rec room," she said. "There'll be a short ride this morning so we can take a look at your riding ability. Then we'll put you into groups for the rest of the camp."

Reese and I left our pyjamas on the bottom bunks, leaving the second top bunk for the latecomer.

"I wonder who we're sharing the cabin with," I said. "I'm really excited to meet new people."

"I just hope they don't snore," said Reese with a laugh.

The rec room was a much larger version of the cabins. Inside, half of it was taken up with worn, comfy-looking sofas that had been arranged in a huge square. A giant-sized low table sat in the centre.

The rest of the room housed tables for pool, table tennis, and air hockey. The wall across from the door held a dartboard and a huge bulletin board. The bulletin board was covered with flyers advertising everything from riding lessons to hoof oil.

Everyone had settled themselves onto the sofas. Sticking with the familiar faces of Matt and Austin, Reese and I squeezed in beside the two boys on a sofa.

Pete and Hannah were standing at the pool table, sorting through a pile of papers.

"This is going to be cool," I said. "Like hanging out at the riding club, only better."

"Yeah, way better, because we don't have to put up with Jessica Coulson and her precious Ripple," said Reese.

"I think you're going to miss her," said Austin with a laugh. "You have way too much fun picking on Jessica."

"Dad asked her if she wanted to come," said Matt, "but Mrs Coulson didn't want Jessica to bring Ripple here."

"What a surprise," Reese said, rolling her eyes. "Oh well. This is more fun for us."

I guessed that Mrs Coulson didn't think that a beach riding camp was good enough for an expensive show horse like Ripple.

"I'm just glad your dad organized this," I told Matt. "I'm so excited to be here."

Pete rapped his knuckles loudly on the pool table to get everyone's attention. "Listen up," he ordered.

As soon as everyone quieted down, Pete started talking. "Welcome, everyone," he began. "I want to explain to you all how the camp is going to work for the next three days. There'll be a riding activity this morning and a beach ride this afternoon. Tomorrow we'll reverse that. On Wednesday, there'll be a race along the beach, with a prize for the winner."

"What's the prize?" asked a short girl with brown plaits.

"I'm glad you asked, Casey," Pete said. He picked up a black and white plastic box from the floor under the table. He opened it and held it up. I could see that the box held a complete set of new grooming equipment. There was a hoofpick, a body brush, a mane and tail comb, a rubber currycomb, and a sweat scraper. There was even a sponge for washing and a paintbrush for painting hooves.

I gazed at the prize. My own grooming equipment was old and worn. But I'd never ridden on a beach before.

"I wish I could win that," I whispered to Reese.

"You could," said Reese.

I shook my head. There was no way I would win against Matt's games horse and Austin's Thoroughbred. One had been trained for speed and the other had been bred for it. Bobby was a great horse and I loved him, but he certainly wasn't fast on his feet.

Pete and Hannah handed out flyers from the pile of paper.

"Please read the safety information carefully," Hannah said as she handed each of us a piece of paper. "We want you to have a good time while you're here, but our first priority is safety. Once you've finished reading, you can get your horses. Put their bridles on, but no saddles, please. There will be an active riding session in the arena in fifteen minutes."

Wondering what "active riding" meant, I bent my head to read the flyer.

Safety Rules

- Riders must always wear helmets and boots while mounted.

- Riders must ride in a safe manner and be considerate of other riders.

- Riders must stay with their group, and listen for and obey the leader's instructions.

- Riders are responsible for the care and welfare of their own horse at all times. This includes cleaning up yards twice daily and making sure your horse has enough hay and fresh water for the time that you're at camp. This also includes cleaning up after yourself while sharing the camp facilities.

- Most of all, riders must have fun and enjoy the camp.

I stuffed the flyer into my shirt pocket and headed out to Bobby's paddock.

No saddles? I thought nervously. I had never ridden bareback in my life. I wasn't even sure I could do it.

"I want everyone to get into four groups,"
yelled Peter.

I steered Bobby into the far-left corner of the
arena. Three other riders followed. Reese, Matt
and Austin were in other corners, but I hadn't
had time to look around for them when Hannah
spoke.

"Those who can mount without stirrups, go
ahead. Everybody else, help each other up. Pete
and I are here to help, too," she called.

I caught a glimpse of Matt effortlessly vaulting up onto Bullet's back.

A couple of the others vaulted, too, but most people had to ask for help. I was basically okay at vaulting – sometimes – but it was still hit and miss. I decided not to risk it.

"Here, let me help you," someone said. I turned. It was Casey, the girl with the plaits. She helped me get onto Bobby's back.

"Thanks a lot," I said, smiling.

"No problem," she said. Then she vaulted onto her own horse.

It felt really strange to be sitting on Bobby without the security of the saddle. I could feel the warmth of his body through the fabric of my jodhpurs. My legs hung down, with no stirrups for support.

I felt like a beginner all over again as I sat on Bobby's back. I kept a firm grip on the reins with one hand, and twisted the other hand into Bobby's thick mane to steady myself.

"This is weird," said Casey. "I feel like I'm going to fall off."

I laughed nervously as the rest of my group agreed.

"Each group can form a circle, but stay in your corner of the arena. Please keep your horses to a walk," Pete called out.

It didn't take long before I started to relax and enjoy the feel of riding bareback. Riders began to loosen up and talk to each other as we walked our horses in a circle.

"I like your horse," someone said. I turned to my right. A pale-skinned girl with braces on her teeth nodded at Bobby and smiled at me.

"Uh, thanks. His name is Bobby," I said. "I like yours, too."

The girl was riding a little bay with two white spots on its hind legs. "I've only had her for a few weeks," said the girl. "Her name is Dazzle. I'm Jodi."

"Who wants to try trotting?" yelled Pete from the other end of the arena.

A cloud of dust rose from the thick sand of the arena's surface as everybody urged their horses into a trot. Trotting while bareback meant that I had to really cling with my legs and keep my body upright to stay in balance.

As I jiggled my way around the circle, I could feel myself slipping sideways. I clamped my legs onto Bobby's sides and tried to push myself back to an upright position.

But Bobby misunderstood. When I squeezed my legs tighter, he thought I wanted him to speed up. He trotted faster.

"No, Bobby, not this time," I muttered.

I tried to slow him down using the reins. But the faster trot had made me lose my balance altogether, and I toppled over Bobby's flanks.

I hit the soft sand of the riding arena. My hip and shoulder landed first. One of my legs was clipped by Bobby's hoof as he moved sideways away from me.

Hannah ran over to me.

"Are you okay?" Hannah asked as I struggled to my feet.

I couldn't catch my breath. I just nodded.

"Maybe you should sit out for the rest of this lesson," said Hannah.

I took a gulp of air and thought about what I should do.

Pete had kept the other three groups going. They were all concentrating on the riding. No one was watching me.

My group, though, had stopped trotting. They were all staring at me.

I thought about sitting out the rest of the session, like Hannah had said. It was tempting, but I didn't want everyone to think I was giving up.

I dusted the sand from my legs. "I'm fine," I said. "Would you please help me back on?"

Hannah grinned. "Good for you," she said. "I like to see people try again when they fall off. You can do it."

Only a few feet away, Bobby stood, patiently waiting. I rubbed the base of his neck near his withers. Then I took the reins and lifted my left leg so that Hannah could boost me back on.

I tried trotting again. Once again, I felt my body begin to slide.

"Oh," I said. "Slow down, Bobby!" I didn't want to fall again.

This time, I quickly brought Bobby back to a walk.

Some of the other riders started to canter after trotting for a while. I watched them, but kept Bobby going at a sedate walking pace.

By the end of the session, my muscles screamed with pain and fatigue. I felt as if I'd fallen off a Clydesdale onto concrete, instead of from a smaller horse onto deep sand.

I leaned forward and whispered into Bobby's ear, "Good boy. We'll get there."

I tried to ignore the fact that I'd been the only one to fall off.

Chapter Four

I met up with the other Ridgeview riders in
the line at lunch. Even though we'd all washed
our hands after putting our horses back in their
paddocks, all of us were covered in dust from the
sandy arena. Especially me.

Hannah stood behind a counter and served
food. I held my plate out, and she piled it high
with potato salad, egg mayo, chips, and two hot
dogs. Pete walked around the tables with a jug,
pouring fruit juice into glasses. I was starving. I
couldn't wait to eat.

I sat down next to Reese. Matt and Austin were across from us.

"What happened to you four?" someone said. "You all look like you've been playing in a sandpit."

I looked up, fork in hand, to see Jessica Coulson standing at the end of the table. As if I didn't already feel dirty and sweaty enough, Jessica's outfit of sandals and a short, floaty summer dress made me feel even grubbier.

I heard Reese groan next to me.

"Wow," said Matt. "Look who's here."

"I didn't know you were coming," I blurted out.

Jessica rolled her eyes at me. "I made my own arrangements to get here," she said. "I need to find my cabin. Mum's just putting Ripple away for me."

Ripple, short for Ripponlea Duchess, was Jessica's very flashy-looking black mare. She was an expensive, fancy horse, and Jessica never let us forget it.

"Shouldn't you be the one doing that?" I asked, but Jessica, ignoring the question, was looking around the room.

"Who's in charge here?" she wanted to know.

Austin pointed across the room to Pete. Jessica left us without a backward glance.

The afternoon ride wasn't supposed to start for another hour, so everybody had some free time after lunch.

"Does anyone want to play pool?" Matt asked, standing up from the table.

"I'll come," said Austin.

Reese hesitated before agreeing. "Yeah, why not," she said, and rose to follow.

"I think I might go back to the cabin," I said, stifling a yawn. The fall had left me drained. I thought I might just lie on my bunk and read for a while. "Can you come and get me for the ride later?" I asked Reese.

"Sure," said Reese.

I found my way to the cabin. I was really looking forward to crawling into bed for a little nap.

I had my hand on the cabin door when Casey appeared beside me.

"Hello! You must be one of my cabinmates," Casey said. She smiled.

"Are you the owner of the striped pyjamas?" I asked.

Casey nodded.

"Then I think I am," I said cheerfully. "It's nice to meet one of my roommates. And I wanted to say thanks for helping me get on my horse this morning. I'm Annie. You're Casey, aren't you?"

"That's me. Do you know who else is staying in this cabin?" Casey asked. She reached to open the door.

"I know one of them," I said. "Reese, the girl I was sitting next to this morning. We both ride at Ridgeview Riding Club and go to Ridgeview High."

"I don't belong to a riding club," said Casey. "But I love riding on the beach. I talked my parents into letting me come here all by myself. They said it was fine but not to expect them to pick me up early if I don't like it." She laughed. Then she said, "Ha! Like that would ever happen."

I laughed, too. I could see that Casey really liked camp so far. My fall that morning was starting to feel like a distant memory.

As I followed Casey into the cabin, I was surprised to see Jessica sitting on the bed. She'd changed into jodhpurs and a pink top.

"Can you believe this?" Jessica demanded even before Casey and I were all the way through the doorway.

"What?" I asked.

"There's no bathroom in the cabin," Jessica said. "We have to walk miles to get to it."

I looked out of the open cabin door. The bathroom building wasn't more than 30 metres away.

"Um, Casey, this is Jessica," I said.

Jessica stood up and looked at Casey. "I was just on my way out," said Jessica.

The door banged behind her as she left the cabin. My attention was drawn back to Casey, who was rummaging through her bag. "I'm sure I packed it," she muttered. "Yes! Here it is." Smiling, Casey pulled an MP3 player and earphones out of the bag.

"It was nice to meet you, Annie," she said. "I'll see you at the beach ride." Then she left.

Finally, I was alone. I lay down on my bed, wincing as my battered muscles took my weight. The cabin was quiet.

It was only now, in the quiet, without the camp noises, that I noticed the sound of distant crashing waves. The sea couldn't be too far away.

As I listened, I thought about Jessica's surprise appearance. She'd obviously got her own way again. I didn't really want to share a cabin with her, but I wasn't surprised that Pete and Hannah had put the Ridgeview Riding Club girls together in one place. They probably thought we were all friends.

Still, I wished they hadn't. Jessica's arrival had taken some of the shine away from the camp.

My last thought as I dozed off was, *I'll just have to stay out of her way.*

If that was even possible.

Chapter Five

I opened my eyes and sat up with a start. It took me a few seconds to realize where I was. Long shadows crept across the floor.

There was something I had to do, but I couldn't remember what it was. I swung my legs over the edge of the bed. Outside a horse neighed. The thought rushed at me – that was it. The beach ride! I didn't see a clock anywhere. I hoped I wasn't too late.

I pulled on my riding boots and hurried out of the cabin.

A group of chattering riders stood around in the parking lot. The horses' coats were dark with sweat. People were dismounting and unsaddling.

I groaned. I'd slept too long and missed the ride. The beach riding was what I was looking forward to most at camp. There were only three scheduled rides on the beach, and now I'd missed one of them.

I cleaned out Bobby's paddock. Then I went back to the cabin to get clean clothes, a towel, and my shampoo and face wash.

I tried to talk myself into a better mood as I walked to the bathroom. *At least I'll get a head start on the others and get to take a shower before they run out of hot water,* I thought.

But however hard I tried, I couldn't shake my bad mood.

I was back in the cabin putting away my things when the door opened.

Reese, Casey, and Jessica trooped in. Suddenly, the cabin was crowded.

Right away, the girls began reaching for clean clothes and slinging towels over their shoulders,

"How long have you been awake?" asked Reese.

I stared at Reese, my anger mounting. "How was the ride?" I snapped.

Casey and Reese both stopped in their tracks at my tone.

Jessica didn't notice. With an armful of clothing, a huge toiletry bag, and a hairdryer perched on top of everything else, Jessica kicked open the door with her foot. The door banged shut behind her after she left.

"What's wrong with you?" asked Reese.

I shook my head slowly. "I can't believe you didn't come and wake me up," I said.

Reese turned to me. "Really? Well I can't believe you're being such an idiot." With an angry frown, Reese scooped up her things and marched out of the cabin.

I suddenly felt embarrassed. I caught Casey watching me.

"Sorry," I said quietly. I tried to grin, but it came out more like a grimace.

"Reese did want to wake you up," Casey said softly. "We came in with Hannah. You were sound asleep. Hannah thought that you should get some rest."

A lump of guilt formed in the pit of my stomach. I should never have yelled at Reese like that.

Miserably, I sank onto my bed.

"See you later," said Casey, leaving me alone in the cabin once more.

* * *

Everyone was hungry at dinnertime. The boys, especially, dug into their bowls of spaghetti and meatballs as if they might never see another meal again.

I wanted to apologize to Reese, but she wasn't giving me the chance. She didn't even eat with our group. Instead, she left me sitting with Jessica, Matt, and Austin and ate her dinner with Casey and some of the others.

It seemed like a lot of new friendships had been made during the beach ride. People were mingling more. After dinner, Matt and Austin went off to the rec room with some boys from their cabin. Even Jessica took off with some people.

I was left alone again. I wandered outside, following the well-lit camp paths to the horse yards.

Bobby nickered as I walked up. I had fed him his evening meal of hay and oats earlier. Still, he nuzzled hopefully at my pockets for a treat.

Jefferson pushed his head over the top of the rail and poked his nose at me. Cruise and Bullet watched curiously.

I noticed Ripple in the paddock next to Bobby's.

"Sorry guys, I'm out of munchies for you tonight," I told the horses. I scratched Bobby's ears affectionately and stared up at the sky. A half-moon peeked through thickening clouds. I couldn't see any stars. The night was warm, but in the distance I heard a rumble of thunder.

I stayed there for a long time, enjoying the sound of the nearby sea.

Finally, I said goodnight to the horses and made my way back to the cabin. The room was silent except for the faint, regular breathing of sleeping bodies. All three beds held shadowy mounds.

Quietly, I slipped into my own bunk and lay still, waiting for sleep to come.

The day that had begun with so much promise had turned sour. I just hoped that the next day would be better.

*Chapter
Six*

I woke up suddenly in the middle of the night. Strong winds were beating against the walls of the cabin. Rain tapped rhythmically on the cabin's roof.

How can the others sleep through all this noise? I wondered.

Then I remembered that the other three girls had a full day of riding, while I'd taken a long nap during the afternoon. Of course they could sleep through the storm. They were exhausted.

A sudden flash of lightning lit up the cabin. Just for a second, I could clearly see the sleeping forms of the other girls.

Only moments later, I sat up quickly when I heard a deafening crack of thunder. The wind had grown stronger. The cabin trembled and creaked.

My mouth was dry. I'd never been comfortable with thunderstorms. They always made me really nervous.

Through the noise of the storm I heard the sound of a horse neighing. Then another horse.

Poor horses, I thought.

Except for one tree, the paddocks had no shelter at all. I could only imagine how terrified the horses must be feeling.

Fighting back my own fear, I left my bed and hunted around in the dark for my boots. I just had to make sure that Bobby was okay.

I had my hand on the door handle when I heard another loud crack.

That didn't sound like thunder, I thought.

There was more neighing. Then another sound: then the unmistakable noise of galloping hooves. I flew out of the door.

Ignoring the stinging rain and struggling to make any speed against the force of the wind, I ran towards the paddocks.

I arrived in time to hear fading hoofbeats and see the outline of two horses as they disappeared around a bend in the driveway.

I began to run after them, then stopped. Trying to catch one horse, let alone two, would be pointless.

Wet strands of hair stuck to my face as I turned back to the paddocks. Then I saw it, and my heart stopped.

My whole body tensed as I saw the heavy branch that had neatly snapped the railings between Bobby and Ripple's paddocks.

Bobby and Ripple were gone.

I didn't wait to see if any other horses were missing. Fighting back tears, I turned sharply and ran to the main house to find Pete and Hannah.

As soon as Hannah heard me say, "Bobby and Ripple are gone," she ran out into the rain.

Pete took me to the rec room and told me to sit while he made me a steaming cup of hot chocolate. "I'll be right back," he said.

I sank into a comfortable couch, still dripping wet.

"Okay, Annie," Pete said, putting the mug in front of me. "Slow down and start again. Tell me exactly what happened."

"I want to go look for them," I said. "Please. Bobby's out there somewhere. I have to find him."

Pete shook his head. "I'm sorry, Annie," he said. "It's not safe. Hannah will look for them. In the meantime, just tell me again what happened."

I burst into tears.

I was still shaking when my cabinmates and Hannah burst through the rec room door a few minutes later.

Jessica stormed in, yelling at the top of her voice. "You idiot!" she screamed at me before the door was even shut. "Why didn't you go after them? If Ripple is hurt, it'll be your fault."

I stared up at Jessica. I had wanted to look for them. Worried tears collected in the corners of my eyes. I couldn't blame Jessica for being upset.

"Shut up, Jessica," Reese ordered.

Pete said, "Okay, let's settle down here. As soon as it's light out, we'll organize a search."

"I doubt they'll go very far," Reese said confidently. "There's only one road up to the camp. Besides, all their friends are here."

Hannah and Pete looked at each other. Jessica noticed.

"What?" she demanded. "What aren't you telling us?"

Hannah hesitated. Then she said, "The horses probably left the road. I doubt they'll stay on the riding trails. It's rough terrain all the way down to the beach. Finding them won't be easy."

"But we will find them, won't we?" I asked in a small voice.

"We'll do everything we can to find them," said Hannah. "That will be our number-one priority." She sighed, and then added, "But I have to warn you, there have been sightings of wild horses in this area lately. If the horses meet up with them, they may stay missing for a very long time."

"Oh, great!" Jessica yelled. Her anger exploded again. "What sort of place are you running here? Why don't you take care of the yards to make sure they're safe for our horses? And why didn't someone warn us that this could happen? This is ridiculous!"

Pete cut in. "Hannah, stop scaring the girls," he said quietly. "I don't believe that rumour about wild horses."

Hannah shook her head. "But what about Misty? How can you explain that?" she asked.

"Who's Misty?" asked Reese.

"She was a young mare who belonged to one of our guests," said Hannah quietly. "She went missing last year and hasn't been seen since." Hannah turned to Pete. "I really think she must have joined the wild horses. What else could have happened to her?"

Pete snorted in disbelief. "More likely some crooks found her and sold her somewhere, no questions asked. Or worse. . ." Pete stopped abruptly.

I tightened my grip on my hot chocolate and shuddered. That couldn't happen to Bobby. I wouldn't let it.

The next day, I could hardly contain
my impatience as I watched the rest of the
camp riders saddle their horses. It was almost
lunchtime, and the search party still hadn't
left yet.

Jessica was in the office with Hannah, trying
to contact her mother to give her the bad news
about Ripple. I refused to call anyone – not yet,
anyway.

They are going to find the horses, I told myself.
Bobby and Ripple will be okay. I would rub my face

into Bobby's luscious mane and scold him for running away, but I wouldn't scold too much. I would just be glad to have him back.

I couldn't wait to see my beloved horse again. I felt terrible that he'd disappeared. I wondered if he was scared, or hungry. Then I decided I should try to not think about it. It made me feel too sad. I'd just focus on finding Bobby.

Hannah came out of the office alone. Then she quickly saddled one of the two horses that Pete had brought up from a yard behind the main house.

Hannah's horse was a heavy Clydesdale with hooves like dinner plates. Pete walked out of the office, checked the girth on a spirited Pinto, and swung himself up into the saddle.

Jessica came into the paddock and stood beside me. Her eyes were red and glazed and the tip of her nose was reddened.

"Half of you can go with Hannah and the other half with me," said Pete. "Please stay with your group. We don't need to have any more lost horses – or riders."

"What about us?" I asked. "Which trail should we search first?"

Pete shook his head sympathetically. "Sorry, Annie," he said. "You and Jessica will have to stay here. You won't be able to keep up with the horses. Besides, someone needs to stick around here, in case the horses return."

Jessica nodded. "That makes sense," she said quietly.

"I'm coming," I said bluntly.

Pete frowned. "No way. I'm sorry, Annie," he said. "I know this is hard on you, and you just want to find Bobby, but it's just too risky. Stay put, and we'll do everything we can to bring your horses back safely."

I watched while the others rode off. After the noise of hoofbeats on the road had faded, and the riders had disappeared from view, I followed Jessica back into the rec room to wait.

It was too quiet in there. I didn't feel like watching TV or playing cards, especially with Jessica. I didn't think I could concentrate long enough to read anything. All I could do was walk around.

Jessica sat down on one of the couches. Ignoring me, she pulled a nail file from her pocket and began working on her manicure.

I couldn't sit still. I paced the room, stopping at the bulletin board to read the flyers.

My eyes skimmed across random phrases such as "Master farrier, willing to travel" and "Qualified Instructor" and "Quiet horse for sale," but I wasn't really paying attention to any of them.

The camp was eerily silent. The only sounds were some birdcalls from outside and the regular scrape of the nail file sliding across Jessica's fingernails.

I looked at Jessica. Her head was bent in concentration. She didn't seem to be aware of anything expect her stupid nails.

"Don't you want to go out and find her?" I asked angrily.

Jessica looked up, bewildered. "Huh?" she asked. "What are you talking about?"

I rolled my eyes. "Ripple," I said. "Remember Ripple? You know, your prize show horse, Ripponlea Duchess. The horse you say you love, the one that wins all those ribbons for you. Don't you even care?"

"Of course I care," said Jessica. "But we couldn't ride out with the other people, so. . ." She shrugged.

"Still, don't you wish you could do something?" I asked.

"I called my mum," Jessica said. "She's driving back. By the time Ripple is found, Mum will be here to take us home." She sighed, and added, "This is so stupid. I should never have come to this dumb camp in the first place. I should have known that this kind of thing would happen."

"But what if they don't find them?" My words tumbled out in a whisper.

"Of course they'll find them," said Jessica firmly, as if trying to convince herself. But her bottom lip trembled.

I pulled my hands out of my pockets. "This is ridiculous. I'm going," I announced.

"Where?" asked Jessica.

But I was already running out of the room as fast as I could. "To find our horses," I yelled as I ran out of the door.

Jessica leaped to her feet and ran after me. "Wait!" she called. "I'm coming with you."

We stopped long enough to grab the horses' halters and lead ropes from where they still hung on the paddock gates. Then we shot off down the driveway.

Chapter Eight

There were a lot of trails that led off the main road and crisscrossed the hills around the camp. From the hoofprints of the horses, I could figure out the way the other riders had gone.

It looked as if one group had taken a trail to the right that went up into the hills, while another group had headed left, down a slope towards the beach.

"We should follow them," Jessica said, pointing to the trail leading down.

I shook my head. "No," I said. "We have a better chance of finding the horses if we take a different trail. I think we should go across here." I pointed to a trail that wound across the top of the hill. "Besides," I added, "we'll have a better chance of spotting the horses from the top of the hill."

"But we could end up lost," Jessica argued.

"Not if we stay on the trail," I told her. "We can just follow it straight back. It'll be easy, you'll see."

Jessica shook her head. "Maybe this isn't a good idea," she said, worry creeping into her voice. "Pete told us to stay put. Maybe we should just do what he says."

I sighed. "Look, I can't sit around and wait for news about Bobby," I told her. "You can stay here if you want, but I'm going to look for my horse. It's up to you."

Without looking back, I started walking. The trees on either side of the trail closed in.

I walked fast, calling out Bobby's name over and over. All I could hope was that he would hear me.

After a moment or two, I heard twigs snapping and the clatter of rolling pebbles as they skittered off the trail. Jessica had decided to follow.

"Hey!" she yelled.

I stopped and turned around when I heard Jessica's voice. I couldn't see her through the trees, but it didn't sound like she was too far behind me.

After a moment, when Jessica didn't appear, I called out, "Where are you?"

"I'm here," she said, stepping into view.

"Well, come on then," I said. "Hurry up."

"There's a fork in the trail," Jessica told me. "You said we wouldn't get lost, but how will we know which way to take if the trail keeps changing?"

"There is?" I said. I had been so worried about covering as much ground as possible that I hadn't noticed the trail splitting into two directions.

I followed the trail back to Jessica. Sure enough, the path branched off in two ways. One continued to go up the hill, while the other tilted downhill.

"Look around for something we can use as a marker," I said.

I scanned the ground, then bent down and picked up a small rock. One end of it tapered into a sharp point. I used the point of the rock to carve a large X into one of the trees that lined the trail.

"There," I said. "If we look for that on our way back, we'll know which way to go to get back to the camp."

"So much for spotting the horses from the top of the hill," snapped Jessica. "There's no view at all. Let's head down, at least."

Jessica eyed the sloping trail. "Maybe we can find the beach and catch up with the others," she added.

I hesitated. We'd been walking for at least an hour, and there was no sign of the horses. Jessica was right about the view from where we were – there was nothing to see.

"Okay then," I agreed. "We'll take the downhill trail and see where we end up."

This time Jessica led the way. The new trail wound steeply downhill. My knees soon began to ache because I had to brace myself against the slope with every step.

A distant roaring became louder as we walked down along the trail.

"We must be getting closer to the beach," said Jessica.

Suddenly, the path widened and the trees thinned. The trail came to an end and Jessica and I found ourselves stepping out of the woods into an open, grassy clearing.

I had to put my hand over my eyes to shield them from the dazzling sunlight after spending so long in the forest. The roaring waves were suddenly deafening.

Jessica stopped walking, and I stepped up beside her. Only a few feet in front of us, the hill dropped steeply away. We were standing on top of a cliff, blue sea spread out before us. No horses. Nothing but water.

Sick with disappointment, I screamed into the wind. "BOBBY! RIPPLE!" I yelled.

Jessica didn't join in. I realized that I hadn't heard her call for Ripple at all since we left the camp. What was the matter with her? Didn't she want to find our horses?

"Jessica, why don't you –" I started.

"Wait. Listen," said Jessica. She held her finger to her lips. "I think I hear something."

I listened.

Beneath the sound of the waves crashing against the rocks came a familiar sound. Jessica grabbed at my arm with excitement.

"Did you hear that?" Jessica yelled. "Do you know what that was?"

"A horse?" I asked. "But where is the sound coming from?"

"It sounds like it's coming from that way, but that can't be right," said Jessica, pointing to the cliff edge.

Cautiously, I moved closer. Directly below us, I saw water. To the left was a long, narrow strip of white sand.

"There's a beach down there," I reported. "Come look."

Jessica hesitated. "Are you sure it's safe? How high up are we?" she asked.

I turned and took Jessica by the arm. "Don't worry," I told Jessica. "We're only about twenty feet up. The horses might be down there. We'll have to look over the edge."

I let go of Jessica's arm and lay down on the rocky ground. Then I inched closer to the side. Lying flat made me feel more secure as I looked down the side of the cliff.

"I can't see anything," I said, squinting down the cliff.

Then I spotted something. "Oh no, Jessica," I said. "Oh no."

"What? What is it?" Jessica asked. She dropped to her knees next to me and peered down, too. She gasped.

Huddled together, with flattened ears and bowed heads, three horses stood on a narrow rock ledge. A rush of relief made my heart flutter as I recognized Bobby's red-tinged mane and ears.

Ripple was there, too, looking wet and dirty and not nearly as pretty and glamorous as she usually did. The third horse was black, like Ripple, but it didn't have white markings on the face and legs and looked like it needed a good meal.

"Whose horse is that?" asked Jessica, puzzled.

I shrugged. "I thought only two escaped from camp," I said.

The horses were surrounded by water. When they heard us, a loud whinny echoed off the rock.

"How on earth did they get down there?" Jessica asked.

"They must have been on the ledge when the tide came in," I said. "The question is, how are we going to get them off it?"

Chapter Nine

"We need to get help," said Jessica. "Pete and Hannah will know what to do. We need to find them."

"But wait," I said. "If we leave the horses, how will we find our way back here again? There must be a way to save them by ourselves. Leaving is too risky."

Jessica stared at me. "I thought you said it would be easy to get back," she said. "You said we'd just follow the path. That's what you said."

"I know I did," I said. "But what if we can't find the same trail again? We can't lose the horses."

"We could wait for the tide to go back out," Jessica suggested.

"That could take hours," I said quietly.

Carefully, I rolled away from the ledge, then rose to a sitting position.

A plan began to form in my mind. It was scary, but it might work.

"There might be a way down to them," I said slowly. "If we can get down there, I think we can do it. Once we get down there, we can ride them off the ledge. Then we can swim them back to the beach."

"But we don't have any tack," said Jessica. "And even if we did, Mum would kill me if I rode through the water in my good saddle."

"We have these!" I said, holding up Bobby's halter and lead.

Jessica rolled her eyes. "Bareback?" she said, tossing her hair behind her ears. "You want us to ride them bareback through the sea with only a halter to control them?"

I tried to keep my voice calm. I didn't want Jessica to see how uncertain I was. Getting Bobby and the other two horses off that ledge was my only thought. My plan was just going to have to work.

"Jessica, do you have any better ideas?" I asked. "Bobby and Ripple are in danger down there. Do you want to see them get hurt? We have to do something, and we have to do it now. Before it's too late."

There was a snort from below. Jessica stared at me. Then she called out, "It's all right, Ripple. We're here. We're coming."

Jessica looked at me. "All right. Let's go," she said.

I nodded and stood up. Then I started looking around, trying to find a way down the cliff.

"We could try it from here," I said.

I pointed to a narrow gully that cut through the rock and wound down the side of the cliff face.

Years of wind and rain had eroded the gully into a series of rolling bumps. That meant that the rock was a little less steep along that part of the cliff. Plus, the rock stuck out in some places, which meant we'd have somewhere to put our feet.

"I don't know. It looks dangerous," said Jessica nervously.

I held up Bobby's lead rope and pointed to the one Jessica held in her hand. "Tie it around your waist," I said. "I'll hold the lead rope up here until you reach the ledge. Then you can guide me on my way down."

Jessica shook her head. "I can't," she said. "I hate climbing. You go first."

I just wanted to get down to Bobby. I didn't care how we did it. I secured the lead rope around my own waist and handed the end of the rope to Jessica.

"Don't let go," I ordered. Then I grabbed a rock and started to carefully ease my way down the side of the cliff face.

Blindly, I felt about with my feet, trying to find a place to put them that was strong enough to hold me.

Stones dug into my hands and stomach as I clung like a spider to the cliff face. I moved slowly down towards the ledge.

The rock, warm from the heat of the sun, made my stomach hot through the fabric of my

T-shirt, but my back was wet and cold from sea spray.

My fingers ached with the effort of holding so much of my weight. My feet struggled to keep my balance.

I could feel Jessica pulling on the rope that was tied around my waist. The rope pulled at my skin, and it hurt, but I was glad it was there. It made me feel safe.

The climb down to the ledge only took me a few minutes, but it seemed like hours. As my feet landed on the wet ledge, the horses crowded around me right away. They almost pushed me into the sea.

Bobby nudged me with his nose. Just then, a giant wave slammed against the ledge, soaking me and the horses.

I didn't care. I was just happy to be with my horse again.

"I made it!" I yelled. I looked up at the cliff's edge and saw Jessica there, looking scared. "You can let go of the rope now," I told her. She dropped it, and it fell onto the ground next to me.

I called up again. I had to yell so that she could hear me over the crashing noise that the waves made.

"Come on down, Jess," I called. "I'll catch you if anything happens." I turned to the horses. They were so nervous. "Whoa, guys," I murmured softly. Then I reached out a hand to stroke first Bobby's neck, then Ripple's.

I wanted to hug my horse, and then check him over for any signs of injury. But that would have to wait. I had to help Jessica first.

I looked over at the black horse.

The unfamiliar horse edged back as far away from me as the small space on the ledge would let it. The horse looked even thinner up close. I could have counted every one of its ribs. Its coat was dull and covered in scrapes and scratches. The whites of its eyes showed clearly.

I could tell it was afraid. I felt horrible for the poor thing.

I looked up again to see Jessica's legs coming slowly down the cliff face. Jessica was as pale as the foam on the waves as she slowly climbed down.

I stood hard up against the cliff and waited to catch hold of Jessica's legs. I stretched up my arms and grabbed Jessica's knees.

My own knees wobbled under the weight of the other girl, but I steadied myself. I dug my fingers into the fabric of Jessica's jeans and held on.

"Ouch," Jessica complained. "You're pinching me."

"Hurry up," I said. "Let go of the rock and jump down. I've got you."

Jessica peered down at me for a second. Then she jumped.

My legs buckled under the sudden weight. My foot slipped on the wet rock and I stumbled. Jessica came tumbling down on top of me.

"Aaaahhh!" Jessica screamed, clutching her ankle. "I think something snapped," she sobbed. "It really, really hurts."

"Oh no," I whispered.

The horses had stepped away in alarm as we fell. All three of them were now backed up against the cliff face, watching us.

Ripple and Bobby recovered quickly from their fright. In seconds, both horses had their ears pricked, curious. The black horse's ears were laid flat back against its head.

I untangled myself from Jessica. She started trying to take her boot off.

"Don't do that!" I yelled.

Jessica let go of her boot and stared at me. "It hurts," she said. "I just want to look at it and see if it's broken."

I shook my head. "You should leave it alone," I said.

"What, are you a doctor now?" Jessica asked, rolling her eyes. "I wasn't aware that you'd finished medical school before you started at Ridgeview High."

Two years ago, before I had moved to Ridgeview, I went to a first-aid class with my mother. For some reason I remembered what the teacher had said about broken bones and sprains.

"Actually, I took a first-aid class once," I told Jessica. "They said that if you think you have a broken bone or a sprain, you should stay still. Obviously you won't be able to do that. But they also said that if you take off the clothing around the injury, it'll start to swell."

"So what?" Jessica asked.

"So that will make it worse," I said. "Seriously, just trust me on this one. Can you put up with it until we get back to the camp?"

Jessica winced, but nodded. "I think so. So now what do we do?" she asked.

I didn't want to admit it, but I was beginning to think that Jessica's idea of going for help had probably been the right one.

Ripple stepped forward and pushed her muzzle against Jessica, who reached up and clutched at Ripple's mane.

Using the mane to steady herself, Jessica dragged herself up. She stood beside the horse, putting all her weight onto her good leg.

"Easy, girl," she cooed gently, rubbing Ripple's face.

I watched in surprise. I'd never seen Jessica be so affectionate with her horse. Maybe she wasn't only interested in winning ribbons. Maybe she really did care about Ripple, the same way that I cared about Bobby.

"Let's get the halters on," I said, slipping Bobby's over his ears and securing the buckle.

My fingers were wet and shaking, making it difficult to secure the halter. I tried to calm myself down.

I can do this, I thought. *I can do this.*

Once the buckle was in place, I tossed the loose end of the lead rope over Bobby's neck and pushed it through the other side of the halter to form reins.

I looked up and saw that Jessica was doing the same thing with Ripple's halter and lead.

I helped Jessica onto Ripple's wet, salty back. She winced when her ankle moved, but she didn't complain.

Then, without even thinking about it, I vaulted onto Bobby's back. Jessica shot me a look of admiration, and I felt really proud of myself.

The horses stood still. Both Bobby and Ripple seemed to be waiting for direction from their riders.

"What about the other one?" Jessica asked, motioning to the other horse. "Do you think it will follow us?"

I glanced at the frightened horse. It would be hard enough trying to control our own horses through the waves. I knew I couldn't do anything to help the other horse. It would have to take care of itself.

"Let's hope so," I answered. "We can't ride three horses at once."

Then I remembered something that had been bothering me. "By the way, Jessica, can you swim?" I asked.

Jessica shrugged, which wasn't exactly the answer I had wanted. But there was nothing I could do about that now. There was only one way off this ledge.

Chapter Ten

Pushing firmly against Bobby's sides, I urged him to take the frightening plunge into the water. Bobby didn't want to move.

I thought of the many times Bobby and I had trained at the water jump on the cross-country course at the riding club. I willed myself to calm my own nerves and treat this situation the same way.

"Come on, Bobby," I yelled into the wind as I squeezed my legs against him. "We can do this, boy. It's just another water jump."

I felt Bobby's muscles tense beneath me. Then he launched himself into the sea with a huge leap. I felt myself slipping off his back before we hit the water.

Desperately, I clutched the rope reins, and we came up swimming together. Bobby carried his head high to keep his nostrils out of the water. His legs pumped through the water. I floated at his shoulder.

Jessica and Ripple were still on the ledge, but I was powerless to wait for them as the force of the sea carried me and Bobby away from the ledge.

Now that we were actually off the ledge and swimming, I told myself that things would be all right as long as we kept moving towards the shore. The noise of the waves was quieter now that we were away from the ledge.

I heard a faint scream and looked back to see Jessica and Ripple behind me. Jessica, too, had slipped off Ripple's back and was being towed through the sea by her horse's lead rope.

I heard neighing and looked back. The ledge was disappearing fast as we got closer to the shore. The black horse, left behind, paced the rock. It was calling for Bobby and Ripple, its new friends.

"Come on," I called, even though I doubted the horse would hear me now. "Come on. You can follow us."

At that moment, my view of the horse disappeared as I was swamped by a wave. The giant wave pushed me off Bobby's back. Bobby's legs kept pushing through the water. Panicked, I clung to the rope. My chilled fingers twisted themselves into Bobby's mane.

I may have rescued Bobby from that ledge, but now he was rescuing me. He was pulling me through the water towards shore.

The motion of Bobby's legs suddenly changed

as his hooves touched sand. I didn't stand up quickly enough and found myself dragged on my stomach up the beach for a few feet before Bobby stopped.

Exhausted, sides heaving and gleaming wet, Bobby's nose dropped almost to the sand while he struggled to catch his breath.

My fingers had stiffened into claws. It took a while before I could let go of the lead rope and raise myself to my feet.

Jessica and Ripple appeared a short way up the beach. Ripple, who looked just as worn out as Bobby was, stopped a few strides out of the water. Jessica flopped onto the sand and sat with her head between her knees.

I gulped in mouthfuls of air as I moved up the beach towards Jessica. I gazed out to sea, trying to spot the black horse, but it was useless. The rock ledge was now just a dot on the cliff.

I sat down on the beach beside Jessica. Soaked to the skin and shivering, neither of us spoke for a few moments.

"How's your foot?" I finally asked.

Jessica shrugged. "Sore," she said. "And cold now that my boots are wet." Jessica reached up to stroke Ripple's face. "I didn't know horses were such good swimmers," she added.

"Thank goodness they are," I said. I smiled even though my muscles hurt. Then I frowned. "What should we do about the other horse?" I asked.

Staring out to sea, Jessica began to laugh.

"It's not funny," I said. "That poor horse is all alone out there, and it's scared."

Jessica poked my arm and pointed. "We won't have to do anything," she said. "It's coming straight to us."

Sure enough, there was something dark bobbing through the waves. It was getting closer by the second. When the horse finally lurched its way onto the shore, it stopped and shook before letting out a relieved neigh and trotting over to join Ripple and Bobby.

"Hey," I said, grinning.

The horses nickered soft greetings and craned their necks to sniff each other.

Suddenly, I felt a heavy weight lift from me. We were back on dry land and all in one piece – well, almost, if I didn't count Jessica's sprained ankle.

I looked over at Jessica. Her pale yellow T-shirt had been torn on one sleeve, and a long dark stain ran down the front of it. I had never seen Jessica looking so messy.

"Wow, you look like a model," I said, with a weak giggle.

"Yeah, well, you look like you just lost the jump-off at the Olympics!" replied Jessica.

I rose to my feet. My wet jeans made it hard to move freely. Water squelched inside my boots. Covered in sand, I attempted to dust off my legs and backside. The tiny wet grains stuck to my hands.

"Here," said Jessica, again using Ripple to help drag herself up. "Let me try."

Hopping on one foot, Jessica brushed at my legs. She held up her hands, one still holding Ripple's rope lead, in front of her face. They were coated with sand. "Yuck," she squealed.

I reached down and picked up a handful of sand and stuffed it down the back of Jessica's T-shirt. Jessica squealed again and nearly fell over.

"Oh!" I yelled. "Oh, Jess, I'm sorry." For a second I had forgotten about Jessica's ankle.

But Jessica didn't complain. Instead, she scooped up her own handful of sand and rubbed it into my hair.

"Take that," she said.

We looked at each other and giggled. Together we'd found our horses, rescued them, and even collected a new horse on the way.

We were tired, wet, and grubby. I was pretty sure that Jessica was in a lot of pain.

But still, there was a lot to smile about.

Chapter Eleven

The black horse wandered off to the far end of the beach. It called to the others a few times, but it didn't seem to want to come back. Bobby and Ripple fidgeted and tugged at their leads. I knew it was time to leave the beach. We needed to try to find our way back to the camp.

This time it was me who looked to Jessica for help. "I didn't do the beach ride yesterday, but you did. How do we get back from here?" I asked.

Jessica looked worried. "Honestly?" she began. "I wasn't really paying much attention. Actually,

I don't even know if this is the same beach we rode to."

I chewed my lip, thinking. The beach wasn't very long, and most of it was bordered by the rocky cliff. At the far end – where the black horse now stood looking back at us – the rock stopped and the forest started. I pointed.

"The horses must have come in from there," I said. I tugged at Bobby's lead, ready to set off.

"We're not walking, are we?" asked Jessica, looking down at her injured ankle. "I think it would hurt way too much."

"Of course not. You can't," I said. "But do you think you'll be able to ride bareback?"

Jessica shrugged. "Doesn't look like I have a choice," she said.

I once again helped Jessica up onto Ripple's back. I thought about my own soaking footwear. I had no idea how far away from the camp we were, and I didn't feel like taking a long walk in wet boots.

My thoughts went back to my disastrous attempt at bareback riding yesterday morning. I didn't want to admit to Jessica that I was afraid, especially since she was being so brave about her ankle.

"Can you get on by yourself again?" asked Jessica.

I looked at the expanse of soft sand around us. There was nothing to use as a mounting block.

The constant sea breeze had dried Bobby's coat, although the hair was stiff and rough from sea salt. At least I wouldn't have to worry about him being too slippery.

I grabbed a handful of Bobby's mane and put my hands on top of my horse. Using my arms to take most of my weight, I jumped up and pulled myself over Bobby. At the same time, I lifted my right leg and hooked it carefully over my horse's hipbone.

Just at that moment, the black horse called out again. Bobby's head shot up with a loud answering neigh, and he stepped forward right away.

I found myself on my back in the sand. Jessica, who was watching, tried to hide her big grin.

"If you think it's so easy, maybe you should get off and try it yourself," I told her, standing up and brushing the sand off my trousers.

Jessica's smile vanished. "I'm really sorry, Annie," she said. "It just looked funny. Here, give me Bobby's lead. I'll hold him while you give it another try."

Jessica moved Ripple to stand head to head with Bobby. She leaned forward and grabbed hold of Bobby's lead while I got myself back into position and leapt up again.

This time, Bobby stood still. I pulled myself upright and wiggled to find a comfortable position on Bobby's back. Jessica let go of the lead, which was still knotted to act as a set of reins.

"We'd better keep to a walk so we can look out for hoof prints," I said.

Jessica nodded.

It crossed my mind that I had never before seen Jessica so agreeable. Being injured had brought out the best in her. Or perhaps she was no more confident about this bareback riding thing than I was.

Maybe she thought I was the expert. The thought made me want to laugh. I was about as far from being an expert at bareback riding as you could possibly be. I hadn't even done it once without falling. I tried to push the worry out of my mind. It was the only choice we had.

Another neigh from the black horse carried across the wind. It seemed to be waiting for us to lead the way.

"Okay, we're coming," I called to him. "Hold your horses."

Jessica laughed. Then each of us gave our horse's side a tentative nudge. The horses moved off at a sedate, slow walk. They walked up to the black horse, who greeted them with a relieved nicker.

"Looks like it's attached to us," said Jessica, studying the horse with interest as we continued up the beach. "You know, it looks a little ragged right now," she added, "but I bet if we cleaned it up and gave it a nice big meal, it could be a show horse."

"I wonder where it came from," I said.

Jessica shrugged. "I don't know," she said. "I don't think it's a wild horse. It seems way too well-bred."

"Maybe," I said.

Still keeping the pace to a slow walk, we headed towards the trees. Bobby and I took the lead. Jessica and Ripple were right behind us. Not far behind, the black horse followed slowly.

I could see a faint, narrow trail that led into the forest.

I steered Bobby towards the trail, beckoning for Jessica and Ripple to follow.

We headed into the forest, and the trees thickened around us.

Chapter Twelve

As I got used to the feeling of riding without a saddle, my body relaxed. My jeans were still damp, but I found myself beginning to enjoy the feeling of closeness with my horse that riding bareback gave me. My hips moved in unison with Bobby's as he walked along.

After a while, my balance improved enough for me to untangle my fingers from the hold they had on Bobby's mane. I kept my legs clamped on Bobby's sides, but twisted my upper body a little to look behind me.

"You okay?" I asked, startling Jessica, who seemed to have been in the middle of some kind of daydream.

Ripple pricked her ears at the sound of my voice, then swivelled them backwards and forwards. It was like she was listening in on the conversation.

The black horse had slowed down a little bit. Once in a while, it stopped to snatch a mouthful of the grass that grew along the sides of the path, but it seemed to be anxious to keep its new friends within sight.

"I'm fine, just a little bit sore," said Jessica. Then she asked, "Have you ridden bareback much before?"

"Only at the camp on the first morning," I said. "To tell you the truth, I wasn't very good at it. I fell off right away, and I never really figured out how to do it right."

"It's an odd feeling," Jessica said. "I wasn't sure when I first got on, but I think I'm getting used to it now. How far away from the camp do you think we are?"

I looked around, trying to see something that I recognized. But all I could see was the trail and the trees.

I looked up at the sky and then down at the lengthening shadows on the trail. It was getting late. The thought of being on an unfamiliar trail in the middle of the woods at night was really scary. I shortened my reins and gently squeezed Bobby's sides until the horse changed his gait to a trot.

"We'd better get a move on if we want to find the camp before dark. Can you trot?" I called back to Jessica.

Ripple trotted after Bobby. Jessica had no choice but to hang on and stick with the little mare.

It was a bumpy ride, but I sat up tall and used my seat and legs to stay balanced, just like my dressage instructor, Erica, was always telling me to. I could hear Ripple's hoofbeats loudly tapping on the path behind me. While we'd been walking, I had heard some quiet birdcalls. Now the horses' hooves drowned out the forest noises.

Jessica didn't complain at all. I felt a little guilty about making her trot with her sore ankle. But we'd both be in bigger trouble if we didn't find our way back to camp soon.

I was starting to get really tired. I was thinking of bringing Bobby back to a walk when the sudden sound of a car engine whizzing by broke through the clatter.

"Hey!" both of us shouted.

The car did not stop. It didn't matter. There was only one road up into the hills. *We must be near the camp at last,* I thought.

Before either of us could say anything, a horse neighed somewhere not too far way. Hearing the neigh, the other horse we'd found trumpeted a reply. It came thundering up the trail behind us.

I dropped the rope reins in surprise and was almost knocked off Bobby as the black horse squeezed past me on the narrow path. It galloped on ahead. I felt Bobby step up his pace, then break into a canter.

"WHOA, BOY!" I called.

All in a split second, I scrambled to pick up the dangling rope reins and stay upright on his back. Somehow I managed to stay mounted while Bobby raced after the black horse.

I pulled on the halter with my rope reins. Without a bit, my pulling didn't do much. Bobby slowed down, but only for a second. Soon he was speeding up again to stay close to the black horse.

I could hear Jessica yelling from behind me, but I had no time to say anything. It was all I could do to wrap my legs tighter around Bobby's sides and hang on.

The trail ended. The black horse veered sharply to the left, and Bobby followed. The turn was too much.

I was exhausted. My tired legs couldn't hold on any longer. As Bobby swerved around the bend, I felt myself sliding off his back.

The next thing I knew, I was sitting on the side of the road.

I jumped up to run after Bobby. But before I could move, a figure stepped out onto the road in front of him.

The sight of another human seemed to settle the horse. He slowed to a trot. The figure moved up beside my chestnut horse and grabbed his halter.

Up ahead, the distinctive "Seahorse Stables" sign at the entrance to the camp swayed in the wind.

I heard a horse coming up behind me. It was Ripple, being led by Jessica. She was limping, but I could tell she was as glad as I was that we'd made it back to Seahorse Stables.

I could see now that the figure holding onto Bobby was Pete. Bobby was calming down. He walked along quietly beside Pete as he came back down the road towards us.

"Are you okay?" Jessica asked me.

I nodded, rubbing at a sore spot on my backside. "At least Ripple had enough sense not to take off," I said, frowning at Bobby.

"Actually, she did try," said Jessica. "I got off before I fell off. That was pretty good bareback riding on your part, you know. Even Matt would have been impressed."

I flushed. The truth was, I hadn't had time to think much about it. "It was more like I was just hanging on no matter what," I answered truthfully.

Then Pete reached us. "Where on earth have you two been?" he asked.

It was pretty obvious that he was angry. Jessica and I looked at each other, and then back at Pete.

It seemed like we had some explaining to do.

When the search party had returned to camp to find me and Jessica missing, the alarm had been raised. Everyone was relieved when we showed up safe.

Matt and Austin wanted to hear all about the horses' rescue, but that couldn't happen before Jessica and I were called to the office.

"What were you thinking?" Pete yelled as soon as we walked into the room. "Don't you know what could have happened out there?"

Hannah laid a hand on his shoulder. "Girls, we didn't ask you to stay at camp as a punishment," she said. "Your safety is our first concern."

"It was my fault," I said. "I made Jessica come with me."

"You didn't make me do anything," Jessica said. "I wanted to go."

"Still," said Pete, "you're lucky you came back when you did. We were just about to call the police and your parents."

Hannah interrupted him. "Where did you find the horses?" she asked.

We told them what had happened. By the end of the story, Pete didn't look as mad – but I could tell he still wasn't happy with us.

After Pete and Hannah let us go, Jessica and I made sure our horses were secured in new yards, along with their new friend, the black horse.

Someone had rubbed down and brushed the horses and left them with a huge pile of hay.

Then Hannah marched us off for a dinner of chicken and macaroni cheese. Both of us were starving, but by the time the meal was over my eyelids drooped with fatigue.

Jessica had her ankle checked by the local doctor and was ordered to sleep in the camp infirmary so she wouldn't be disturbed.

I dragged myself off to take a shower. While I was brushing my teeth, I realized that I hadn't seen Reese.

Sadness washed over me. Reese must still be angry over my stupid comments from the day before. After all that had happened, our argument seemed like a lifetime ago. I would have given anything to take back that stupid remark I'd made to Reese. Now it seemed like I'd never get my friend back because of it.

Dressed in pyjamas, I picked my way along the shadowy path from the showers to my cabin. The lights were out. Reese and Casey seemed to be sound asleep.

I thought about waking Reese up to apologize, but decided not to. It was pretty clear that Reese was still mad at me, and I knew she wouldn't want me to wake her up. Besides, I was exhausted. All I wanted to do was to crawl quietly into my bed.

I left my toiletries on the floor, climbed over the foot of the bed and reached up for my pillow. Paper crackled against my leg. I kicked it onto the floor, climbed under the covers, and was instantly asleep.

* * *

I woke the next morning to an empty cabin. Neatly packed bags sat on both Reese and Casey's beds. It was the last day of camp. We'd all be leaving for home after the beach race that afternoon. Jessica's gear was still packed in the cabin lockers.

I dressed and hurried outside. Like Jessica, I figured I could pack up my things later.

First I checked on the paddocks and said good morning to Bobby, Ripple, and the black horse.

The other riders were having a riding lesson with Hannah in the arena. Reese was listening intently to Hannah and didn't look my way.

Once again, I had overslept. But this time, I didn't care that I was missing out. I was happy to save all my and Bobby's energy for the beach race later that afternoon. I went to find Jessica.

Jessica was sitting on a sofa in the rec room. Her bandaged ankle was raised up onto a chair. Jessica's mother sat beside her. They were arguing.

"What's the big deal, Mum? Why can't we just stay until after the race?" Jessica asked in a whiny tone. She stopped talking as soon as she saw me.

"Hello, Annie," Mrs Coulson said coldly.

I dropped my eyes and mumbled, "Hello."

Mrs Coulson stood up. "I'm going to the paddocks to get your gear," she told Jessica. "We'll be leaving right after lunch."

Jessica made a face at her mother's back as Mrs Coulson left the room.

I sat down across from Jessica. "Does your mother blame me for what happened?" I asked, pointing to Jessica's bandaged ankle.

Jessica rolled her eyes. "Probably. She's not too happy with me, either. Ripple and I were entered in the Kerrisdale show next week." Jessica glanced down at her ankle. "Obviously, I can't go now."

"What did the doctor say?" I asked.

"It's just sprained," Jessica told me. "I can't ride for at least two weeks."

"That's too bad," I said. "I'm really sorry."

Jessica shrugged. "Thanks for the advice about not taking my boot off. The doctor said that was the right thing to do. It probably made it a lot better."

"I still feel really bad," I said. "If it wasn't for me insisting we go look for the horses, you would never have been hurt."

"No, I wouldn't have. But if we hadn't gone looking for them, they might have drowned on that ledge for all we know," Jessica said.

I nodded. "How's the black horse?" asked Jessica.

"I just checked on it," I said. "It seemed okay."

Jessica leant forward to adjust the bandage on her ankle.

"I think the doctor must have put this bandage on too tight," Jessica complained loudly.

I stifled a grin. The bandage looked fine to me. This was more like the Jessica I knew. Not the calm, agreeable girl from yesterday.

Pete popped his head through the rec room door. "Did you two hear the news about that horse you came back with?" he asked.

"What news?" asked Jessica.

"Well," said Pete, "I checked her over this morning, and I'm one hundred per cent sure that she's our missing horse."

"Misty!" I said.

"Exactly," said Pete. "So I called her owner, and she's coming right over to get her."

Jessica sniffed. "Well, I hope that girl is grateful. We certainly went to enough trouble to bring her horse back to her safe and sound," she said.

I opened my mouth to remind Jessica that Misty had just followed us home. But instead, I said, "Mrs Moriarty is taking Bobby home, but my parents are driving up to get me. They said they wanted a day out. Do you want to stay and watch the race? You can come home with us this afternoon."

Jessica smiled. "I'd love that," she said. "Thanks." Then she frowned and added, "I think your parents should let me sit in the front seat, though. After all, I'm injured."

I laughed. Some things never change.

I urged Bobby downhill along a dusty trail. Ahead of us was the beach where the race would take place. Bobby and I followed the others down onto the beach.

It had turned into a nice day. The waves rolling onto the shore were smaller and quieter than the day before. The sun's rays pierced the fabric of my top, warming my shoulders.

All of the riders assembled on the beach. Pete had driven Jessica there in his 4×4. The two of them and Hannah sat in deckchairs, set back away from the water. A bright red clipboard lay on the sand at Pete's feet.

A series of plastic orange cones had been placed along the beach. There were four of them, spaced apart. I guessed they were meant as some kind of markers for the race.

I was looking forward to the beach race. Now that we were off the trail and onto the beach, Bobby seemed to be feeling good, too.

A buzz of anticipation bit through the cool sea breeze. The others were chattering excitedly. Despite my burst of energy, I knew I didn't have much of a chance at winning the grooming kit. Everyone else wanted to win just as much as I did.

Austin was having trouble with Cruise. Normally well-behaved, the mare was anxiously looking out over the vast expanse of sea and bounding up and down on her forelegs. Austin, who was usually so cool, was looking flustered.

The deep sand of the beach and the open water would be strange to Cruise, who was used to living in a very controlled environment of stables and small paddocks.

Reese was ignoring everyone. She'd taken Jefferson away from the group and was trotting him up and down a short stretch of beach.

Matt sat easily on Bullet, who seemed quite relaxed. Matt was busy talking with a rider that I hadn't got to know.

I sighed. I had hoped to make some new friends at this camp. But between oversleeping on the first afternoon, then searching for my horse the second day, my contact with new people had been limited to Pete and Hannah, Casey, and the girl with the braces, Jodi.

My thoughts were interrupted by Hannah, who rose from her deckchair and took a few steps forward. "Everybody over here so I can explain the rules," she said.

The riders snapped to attention. "You're probably thinking this race is going to be some kind of sprint down the beach, and whoever gets to the finish line first wins," Hannah began.

That was exactly what I'd been thinking. I looked around. Everyone else looked confused, too.

"Not so," called Pete, picking up his clipboard. "For a start, that would be far too dangerous."

Hannah nodded. "Each one of you will be racing individually," she said.

A buzz of whispers ran through the riders. Hannah held her hand up. "We've worked out the distance according to some guidelines about riding to time," she continued. "You will need to figure out how much time it should take from section to section. Pete will be recording all your times. The rider who completes the course in a time that is closest to the time we want will be the winner."

"Most of you will find that the time can be achieved by either a fast trot or a steady canter," Pete said.

"So how will we know if we're going the right speed?" Reese called out.

I had been wondering the same thing. I leant forward to stroke Bobby's neck, all the while listening carefully for Hannah's answer.

Hannah held up one finger. "I'll give you a clue," she said. "Slow and steady wins the race."

Since we all knew that we might be waiting around for some time, the other Ridgeview Riding Club kids and I dismounted until it was our turn to race.

More than once at riding club events, Erica and the other instructors had made a point of telling us not to use our horses as "armchairs" at events. It wasn't fair to the horses, and it wasn't good for us.

Everyone had their own ideas about what speed to travel at. I watched Casey do the whole length of the course in a slow canter, while Matt began at a slow trot for the first leg. Bullet struggled for a free rein, but Matt held him firmly. He allowed the horse to go a little faster for the second leg and then broke into a controlled canter for the last.

The next rider, Austin, totally lost it. The way Cruise took off, anyone would have thought she was training for the Olympics. Austin tried to keep her in check and managed to finally stop her way down the beach, way past the finishing cone. Afterwards he walked the excited, sweaty mare back to the group, shaking his head and frowning.

"Crazy Thoroughbred," I heard him mutter as he rode back past me.

I decided to follow Matt's example. I kept Bobby moving in a rhythmic trot, and very gradually asked him to increase his speed. As I passed the third cone, Bobby broke into a canter.

"Go for it, Annie," a voice called.

Jessica? I thought with surprise, but I was busy racing, and I forgot about it pretty fast. I was focused on riding. I tried to pay attention to Bobby's speed and keep him on track.

I had no idea if we were going at the right speed or not, but it felt good. I loved riding on the beach, and that was all that mattered.

The rest of the riders went through. Each person seemed to have their own ideas about what would be the best time. Some people went pretty slow. Some people went really fast. Some people did the first leg really slowly and the last leg fast. Without a watch to time everyone, I guessed that the speeds varied quite a bit. I just hoped mine was the one that was right, but I didn't think it would be. That was okay.

Reese and Jefferson were the last pair to ride.

"Good luck," I called out as Reese guided her horse to the start. Reese rode on without even turning around.

That hurt. Reese was acting as if I didn't even exist. As if we'd never been friends at all.

Chapter Fifteen

Feeling sad, I dismounted to watch Reese ride the course. Pete called out, "Go!"

Jefferson moved past the first cone in a steady trot. Just like I had, Reese gradually increased her speed as she passed each cone. I glanced over at Hannah who was watching Reese.

As Jefferson cantered back after finishing the course, Hannah nodded happily. She turned to speak to Pete. I moved closer and caught the last few words. "She figured it out," Hannah said.

Pete grinned back at Hannah and wrote something down on his clipboard.

Five minutes later, Pete strolled up to the group of riders. We were all waiting to find out who'd won the race.

"The winner, only one second faster than the optimum time, which was three minutes and ten seconds, is Reese Moriarty!" Pete said.

Everybody clapped. I looked longingly at the grooming kit in Pete's hand. Oh well. I was glad it was going to my friend.

Then I looked at Reese. I wanted to congratulate her. Once again, Reese looked away. She seemed determined not to make eye contact with me.

I rode back to camp in silence. Reese ignored me, riding on ahead of the main group. She had become very friendly with Casey, who shot me a sympathetic look before riding on to join Reese.

The horses clattered through the camp gates. Riders headed their horses in the direction of their individual yards. I noticed a horse trailer parked near the rec room. I guessed that someone else's parents had arrived early.

I removed Bobby's bridle, replacing it with his halter. I cinched up Bobby's girth to release the buckle, then slid the saddle from my horse's back.

Reese was doing the same thing with Jefferson in the next paddock, but she didn't look in my direction.

I returned to the cabin to pack up my things. When the last of my clothes had been stuffed into my bag and the zipper was closed, I hoisted the bag over my shoulders and looked around the cabin one last time.

Camp had been nothing like I'd expected or hoped for. I had fallen off Bobby more than once, slept through half of the first day, lost my horse, and then almost drowned trying to rescue him. Worst of all, Reese was mad at me. I'd had enough. It was time to go home.

A scrap of paper poked out from under my bed. I reached down, picked it up, and was about to toss it into the garbage when I caught sight of a single, handwritten word.

Annie

I froze when I recognized Reese's handwriting. The note was meant for me. Then I remembered kicking paper off my bed in the dark the night before.

With shaking fingers, I unfolded the note and began to read.

* * *

I found my parents in the rec room and we all hugged. I made sure that it was okay to give Jessica a ride home. Then I went to the car and tossed my bag in the back. A clatter of hooves on wood made me look up.

Pete and Hannah were standing near the horse trailer that I had noticed earlier. The ramp was down, and disappearing into the back of the truck was Misty, the runaway horse.

A slim girl wearing black jodhpurs came down the ramp of the trailer. She shook Pete and Hannah's hands.

Pete saw me and waved me over. "Come here, Annie," he called.

Curious, I walked across the paddock to the truck. The smiling girl rushed up and hugged me warmly.

"Annie, this is Zoe," Pete told me. "Zoe owns Misty, the horse you rescued," he explained.

Zoe let me go and stepped back. "Thank you so much for finding Misty," she said. "I couldn't believe it when I got Pete's call. It was the best day of my life. And please thank your friend, too. I thought I'd lost Misty forever."

"She found us, really. Actually, she found our horses. Then she just followed us home," I said.

"Well, she needs to eat, but I'm lucky that's all that's wrong with her," said Zoe. "Where do you think she could have been living all this time? Some people thought she'd gone off with wild horses. Did you see any?"

I shrugged. "Nope," I told her. "When we found our horses she was there with them."

"I bet someone nearby has had her," Pete said. "Maybe she escaped from them, just like she escaped from here in the first place. But I suppose we'll never know for sure."

Inside the truck, Misty stamped her foot a few times.

"I'd better get going," said Zoe. She pressed a switch on the side of the trailer. With a loud whirring, the ramp began to slowly lift, gradually closing the gap. Misty disappeared from view, and the ramp became a firmly closed door on the back of the trailer.

Zoe climbed up into the cabin and turned the truck's ignition key. The engine roared into life. Zoe leaned out of the window. She was smiling at me and holding out two twenty-pound notes.

"I want to reward you and your friend for finding Misty. Take one and give the other one to her," said Zoe.

I shook my head. "No," I said. "You don't have to do that. Really."

"Please," Zoe said. She leaned further out the window and pressed the money into my hand. "I really want you to have it. I mean it. It's the least I can do."

My fingers closed over the money. I could see that Zoe wouldn't be happy until I took it.

"Well, thanks," I said.

"I'm the one who should be thanking you," said Zoe. "I have my horse back, and I'm the happiest person in the world."

Zoe waved. Then she turned the truck and headed down the driveway.

Only seconds after Zoe's truck left, Mrs Moriarty arrived. She waved to me as she backed the 4×4 up to the horse trailer.

I made my way into the rec room. It was crowded. People had changed out of their riding clothes.

Jessica sat on one of the couches, her foot still bandaged. She wore a white tank top over a pretty little red skirt. A matching red cardigan topped the outfit. She looked totally out of place among all of the people wearing practical jeans and polar fleece sweatshirts.

I handed Jessica twenty pounds. "It's our reward for finding Misty," I explained.

Jessica took the money and stuffed it into her pocket. "Good," she said smugly.

I stared at Jessica. She was such a brat!

I wondered what Jessica, who always had the best of everything, would spend the twenty pounds on.

I knew exactly how I was going to use the money – I had known from the moment Zoe had given it to me. Twenty pounds was more than enough for a new grooming kit. And I could buy Bobby some hay with the change.

"My parents are here," I told her. "We'll be ready to leave soon." Then I walked away.

My eyes scanned the room, looking for one person in particular. Finally, I spotted Reese across the room.

"Reese!" I called my friend's name out loud as I pushed through the crowd to stand in front of her.

Reese had been talking with Matt and Austin. I reached out and hugged Reese. She stood stiffly. Instead of lifting her arms to return my hug, she kept her arms firmly at her sides.

"I thought you were still angry with me," I explained. "And I didn't find your note until this morning. I'm so sorry I snapped at you."

In her note, Reese had explained everything. She'd been mad at me at first, but then she was so scared when I was missing, and she realized that our fight was stupid. She'd apologized.

I felt Reese's body soften. I stepped back and looked at my friend.

Reese's eyes were watering. "When you went missing with Jessica, I was so worried," she said. Her words came out in a whisper. "And then when you didn't say anything today, I thought you weren't speaking to me. I thought you'd seen my note, and it didn't matter."

I leant forward and hugged my friend again. "I thought you weren't speaking to me!" I told her.

Matt and Austin coughed in unison. "Can you two quit the mushy stuff?" Matt said. He was grinning.

I let go of Reese. "Hey, Reese," I said. "Why don't you come home in my car for a change? Our mums can take the horses home together."

Reese hesitated.

"Come on," I said. "It's a long drive. You can't leave me with Jessica Coulson on my own. We've already spent enough time alone together."

Reese shrugged, pretending to think about it. "Does that mean I'll have to listen to Jessica complain all the way home?" she demanded.

I nodded. "Probably, but we'll let Jessica sit in the front with my dad," I said. "By the time we get home, she'll know all about the estate agents in Ridgeview, and he'll know exactly how many ribbons Jessica has won and what each one was for."

"Now, that is just mean," said Reese with a laugh. "Okay. Now, start from the beginning, and tell me everything. How did you find those horses?"

About the Author

When she was growing up, Bernadette Kelly desperately wanted her own horse. Although she rode other people's horses, she didn't get one of her own until she was an adult. Many years later, she is still obsessed with horses. Luckily, she lives in the country, where there is plenty of room for her four-legged friends. When she's not writing or working with her horses, Bernadette and her daughter compete at riding club competitions.

Horse Tips from Bernadette

- Never ride alone.

- Horses have different needs in different seasons. In colder months, they may not be able to graze much, so they'll need to be fed more. They also need help staying warm. In warm months, they may need more water.

- Horses need to have clean water available at all times.

- Learn everything you can about horses.

For more, visit Bernadette's website at
www.bernadettekelly.com.au/horses

Glossary

- **bareback** without a saddle

- **dressage** method of riding and training a horse to perform

- **farrier** person whose job it is to take care of a horse's hooves and shoes

- **girth** part of a horse's saddle that goes under its stomach to secure the saddle

- **jodhpurs** trousers worn for horse riding

- **mount** get on a horse

- **paddock** enclosed area where horses can graze or exercise

- **stirrups** rings or loops that hang down from saddles to hold riders' feet

- **tack** equipment that you need to ride a horse

- **Thoroughbred** breed of English horses developed especially for racing

Advice from Annie

Dear Annie,

There's this girl at school who's always really mean to me. Next week, we're stuck working on an assignment together. How can I get this done and get a good mark, but not get in her way?

Sincerely,

Bullied in Bolton

Dear Bullied in Bolton,

I have totally been there. Sometimes girls can be so mean to each other. It would be great if we were all kind all the time, but in real life, that doesn't happen, does it?

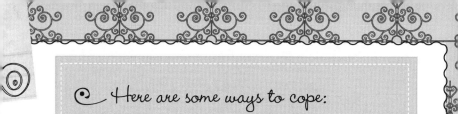

◎ Here are some ways to cope:

1. *Be yourself.* Don't let the bully change you. You're you, and you're great.

2. *Be smart.* Sometimes it seems like playing dumb and letting another person run the show is your best chance for not getting bossed around or teased. It's not. It'll hurt your chances of getting a good mark, and you'll feel worse in the long run.

3. *Be bold.* Have a great idea for the project? Speak up! Think something might not work? Say so. (But do it kindly.)

4. *Know your limits.* Being yourself, being smart, and being bold doesn't mean you can't get help if someone is treating you badly.

No matter what, do your best. Good luck on your assignment. I bet you'll be great!

Love,
♡ Annie

The Ridgeview Book Club Discussion Guide

Use these reading group questions when you and your friends discuss this book.

1. Talk about Jessica Coulson. How does she change over the course of this book? What does Annie learn about Jessica that surprises her?

2. Annie thought that her holiday would be very different from how it ended up. What parts could she have controlled? What could she have done to change things?

3. All friends argue sometimes. But many arguments can be prevented. What could Annie and Reese have done to stop their fight from happening? What would you have done in the same situation?

The Ridgeview Book Club Journal Prompts

A journal is a private place to record your thoughts and ideas. Use these prompts to get started. If you like, share your writing with your friends.

1. Write about a time you spent away from home. What happened? Where were you? How did you feel?

2. Make a list of places you'd like to travel. What is number one on the list? Why do you want to go there? What would you do there? Plan a fantasy holiday.

3. Friendships have ups and downs. Write about your best friend. How did you meet? What did you think of her when you met? What do you think of her now?

Join the Ridgeview
Riding Club!

Read all of Annie's
adventures.

RIDGEVIEW RIDING CLUB
If Wishes
were Horses
BERNADETTE KELLY

RIDGEVIEW RIDING CLUB
Courage to Ride
BERNADETTE KELLY

RIDGEVIEW RIDING CLUB
Leap of Faith
BERNADETTE KELLY